FOOTBALL

Tanis Booth

Weigl Publishers Inc.

Published by Weigl Publishers Inc.
123 South Broad Street, Box 227
Mankato, MN 56002
USA
Copyright © 2001 Weigl Publishers Inc.
All rights reserved. No part of this publication may be reproduced, stored in a retrieval system, or transmitted in any form or by any means, electronic, mechanical, photocopying, recording, or otherwise, without the prior written permission of Weigl Publishers Inc.

Project Coordinator
Rennay Craats

Layout and Design
Warren Clark

Copy Editor
Heather Kissock

Library of Congress Cataloging-in-Publication Data available upon request from the publisher. Fax (403) 233-7769 for the attention of the Publishing Records Department.

ISBN 1-930954-25-5

Printed in the United States of America

3 4 5 6 7 8 9 05 04 03

Photograph credits
Cover: Visuals Unlimited (H.Q. Stevens); Title: Frozen Motion Phtotography (Bernie Steenbergen); Contents: Reuters/Archive Photos (Mike Blake); Archive Photos: page17R (Morton Tadder); Canadian Football Hall of Fame: page 4; EyeWire: page 21R; Frozen Motion Photography: pages 6 (Bernie Steenbergen), 7L (Bernie Steenbergen), 10B (Bernie Steenbergen), 11R (Bernie Steenbergen), 12R (Bernie Steenbergen); Globe Photos Inc: pages 16L (Bill Crespinel), 16R (Albert Ferreira), 17L (Bill A. Crespinel), 18L (Fitzroy Barrett), 18R (Fitzroy Barrett), 19R (Craig Skinner); Monique de St. Croix: page 7R; Reuters/Archive Photos: pages 14B (Joe Traver), 19L (Eric Miller), 22/23BL (Mike Blake); Visuals Unlimited: pages 5T (E. Webber), 5B (A. Gurmankin), 8 (Hank Andrews), 10T (E. Webber), 11L (Mark. E. Gibson), 12L (Mark. E. Gibson), 13L (H.Q. Stevens), 13R (Mark Newman), 14T (Mark. E. Gibson), 15T (Mark E. Gibson), 15B (H.Q. Stevens), 20L (Cabisco), 20R (Cabisco), 21L (Francis E. Caldwell), 23T (A. Gurmankin), 23BR (H.Q. Stevens).

Every reasonable effort has been made to trace ownership and to obtain permission to reprint copyright material. The publishers would be pleased to have any errors or omissions brought to their attention so that they may be corrected in subsequent printings.

Contents

PAGE 4
What is Football?

PAGE 6
Getting Ready to Play

PAGE 8
The Field

PAGE 10
Keeping Score

PAGE 12
Positions on the Field

PAGE 14
The Super Bowl

PAGE 16
Superstars of the Sport

PAGE 18
Superstars of Today

PAGE 20
Staying Healthy

PAGE 22
Football Brain Teasers

PAGE 24
Glossary / Index

What is Football?

Football probably began in England around 1820. A soccer player got bored with using only his feet to move the ball. The player picked up the ball and ran with it, changing the rules of soccer. This sport became known as rugby. It came to America in 1850.

In rugby, players can both kick and run with the ball. It was played at some East Coast colleges in the United States. Americans made some important changes. They used an egg-shaped ball instead of a round one and kept score differently. Americans renamed this game football. Football is now one of America's favorite sports to play and to watch on television.

Football in the 1800s looked very different from games that are played today.

Football is played by two teams of eleven players. The teams take turns being on offense and defense. When a team is on offense, it is its job to score points. A player can score points by kicking the ball, passing the ball to a teammate further up the field, or running with the ball. The defensive team's job is to stop the other team from scoring points and to keep the ball from moving forward.

The offensive team tries to move the ball up the field. They do this by throwing to a receiver or running with the ball.

A team has four chances to score a **touchdown** or to move the ball ahead enough to get another four chances. Each chance is called a **down**. If the offensive team does not move the ball far enough in four downs, it becomes the other team's turn to try to score points.

Two teams line up facing each other to start the game. This is called the line of scrimmage.

CHECK IT OUT

Read about the history of the National Football League at www.nflhistory.com/roots.shtml

5

Getting Ready to Play

Football teams wear uniforms when they play. They also wear equipment under their uniforms. Football is a rough game, so it is called a **contact sport**. When a player has the ball, there is always an opponent whose job is to take it away. Football equipment is very important because it helps protect a player from injury.

Players wear jerseys with their number on the back. They fit over padding to protect the players. Players wear separate pads for their ribs, arms, and often elbows. This saves their muscles and bones from injury after **tackles**.

Some football players wear gloves. This helps them hold on to the ball. When it is raining, the ball can get slippery.

Football players wear tight-fitting pants so the players are harder to hold on to. These pants fit over padding that protects the player's legs. Players wear thigh and knee padding when they are on the field.

The inside of a football is like a very strong balloon. This balloon is called a bladder and is covered with brown leather – all of this forms a football. On one side of the football are white laces. These laces help the player grip the ball. Gripping the ball is important when a player is trying to throw it a long way.

A helmet and face guard protect the player's head and face. Each helmet has soft padding inside, which adds further protection. The helmet has a face guard to protect a player's eyes, nose, and jaw. A mouth piece must also be worn to protect the player's mouth and teeth.

Footballs come in different sizes for different sized hands.

Players wear shoes called **cleats**. They have spikes, or pieces of plastic, on the bottoms. This helps them grip the ground and not slip on the grass or **turf**.

The Field

A football game takes place on a large, rectangular field. An American football field is 160 feet wide and 360 feet long. Surrounding the rectangle are thick white lines to mark the boundary. The long part of the field is called the **side line**. The short part of the field is called the end line. At each end of the field are goal posts. Goal posts are in the **end zone**. The end zone is where a touchdown is scored.

The Orange Bowl Stadium in Miami is an outdoor football field. It holds 74,000 people.

The two teams switch from being on offense to defense throughout the game. **Possession** of the ball changes from team to team several times during the game. The team with the most points at the end of four fifteen-minute quarters wins the game.

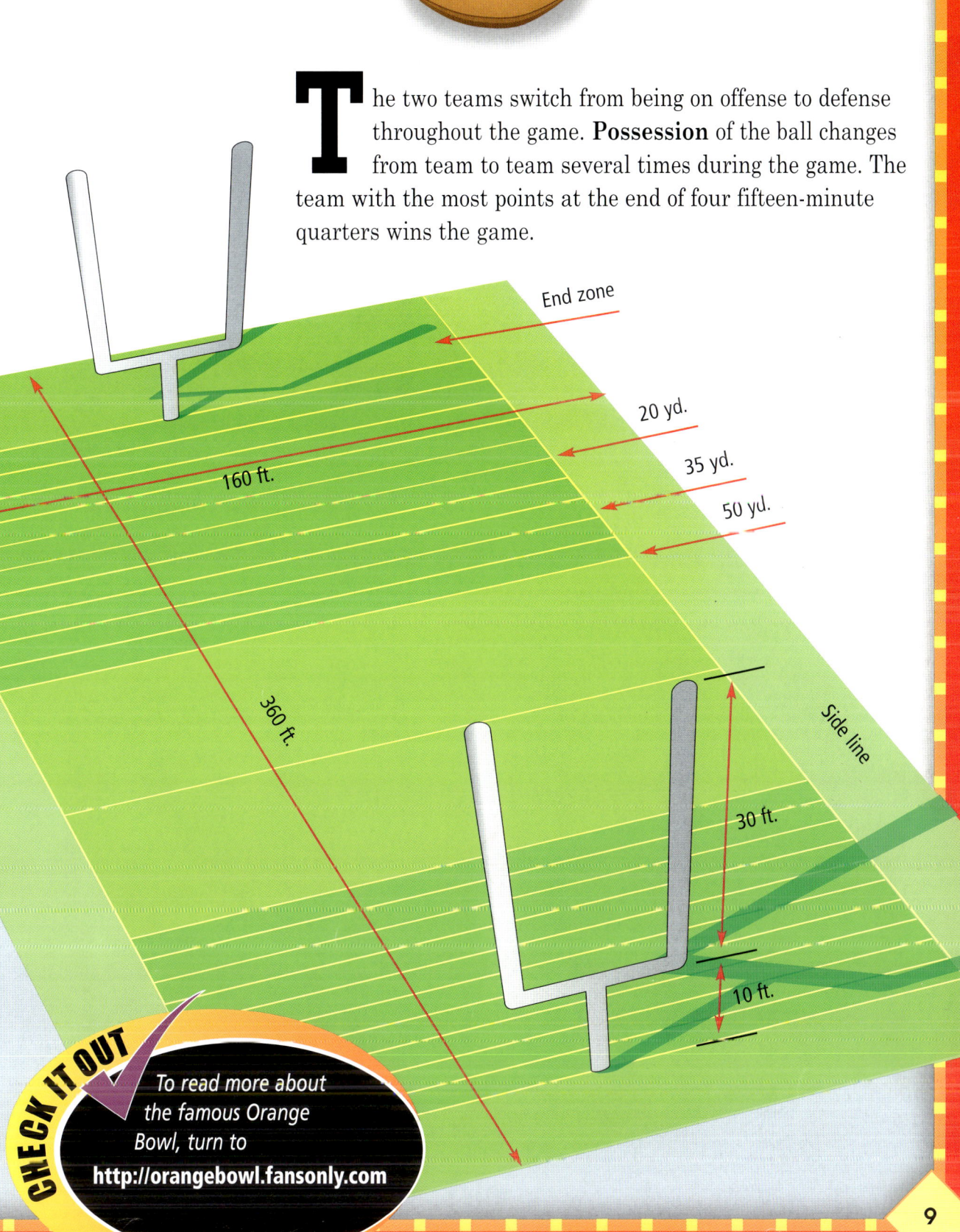

CHECK IT OUT
To read more about the famous Orange Bowl, turn to
http://orangebowl.fansonly.com

Keeping Score

The main goal in football is to score touchdowns. This is achieved when a player runs across the end zone while holding the ball. A player also scores a touchdown if he or she catches the ball in the end zone.

Each team gets four chances, or downs, to score a touchdown. A team must move the ball at least ten **yards** down the field in order to get another four downs. The other team tries to prevent any touchdowns. They tackle players and block the ball. Another way to prevent a touchdown is to catch a pass from the other team. This is called an **interception**. When a player intercepts a ball, his or her team switches from being on defense to offense.

Getting to the ball before the other team takes a lot of effort. Players have to run faster and reach further than their opponents.

A team can also score points by kicking a field goal. After a touchdown, the team can try kicking the ball through the goal posts. The player who kicks the ball is called a place kicker or kicker. The ball must go between the two posts to score points.

A different number of points is given for different ways of scoring. A touchdown is worth six points, a field goal is given three points, and kicking the ball through the goal posts after a touchdown is worth one point.

The officials wait in the end zone when the ball is kicked. They throw their arms up when a field goal is scored.

The kicker only comes on the field when it is time to try to score a field goal.

CHECK IT OUT

For more on football rules, surf over to
www.football.com/rulesandinfo.shtml

11

Positions on the Field

Each team carries approximately forty players. Only eleven players from each team are on the field at once. There are many different positions. Certain skills make players good at certain positions.

Some offensive players are small and fast. They are passed the ball, and they run down the field with it. These players are called receivers. Receivers have very strong leg muscles because they need to reach a top speed quickly and keep that speed for a short time.

Receivers move the ball toward the end zone. They keep the ball tucked close to their bodies. This prevents them from dropping the ball.

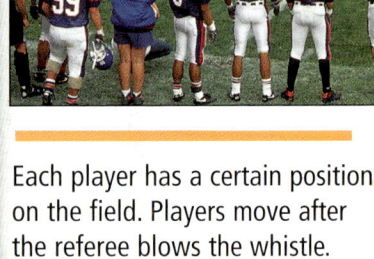

Each player has a certain position on the field. Players move after the referee blows the whistle.

The quarterback is the player who decides the plays for the rest of the team. The team gathers on the field in a tight circle before a play starts. This is called a **huddle**. It is the quarterback's job to call the plays during the huddle and to make sure all of his or her teammates understand the play.

Other players take on defensive positions. They are usually bigger and stronger than offensive players. They are called linesmen. They block or tackle players from the other team. Each offensive and defensive position is broken down into more specific but similar positions.

The quarterback is the player who usually passes the ball. The quarterback requires a lot of skill and accuracy when throwing a football. He or she has to make the ball spin as it flies through the air. This is called a **spiral**.

Players can get hurt when they are tackled.

CHECK IT OUT
Find out more about the ins and outs of football at
http://members.aol.com/msdaizy/sports2/footb1.html

13

The Super Bowl

Children interested in learning to play football join community football teams. They can also play on junior and senior high school teams. From there, many try out for college or university teams. College players compete in the National College Athletic Association (NCAA).

College football is very similar to the National Football League (NFL) but has a few differences in scoring. Colleges also have wider goal posts. The college championship game is called the Orange Bowl. Winning the Orange Bowl can draw the attention of professional teams to young players.

Many young athletes start out playing football in the school yard.

The competition in the Super Bowl is fierce. Players do all they can to win the game.

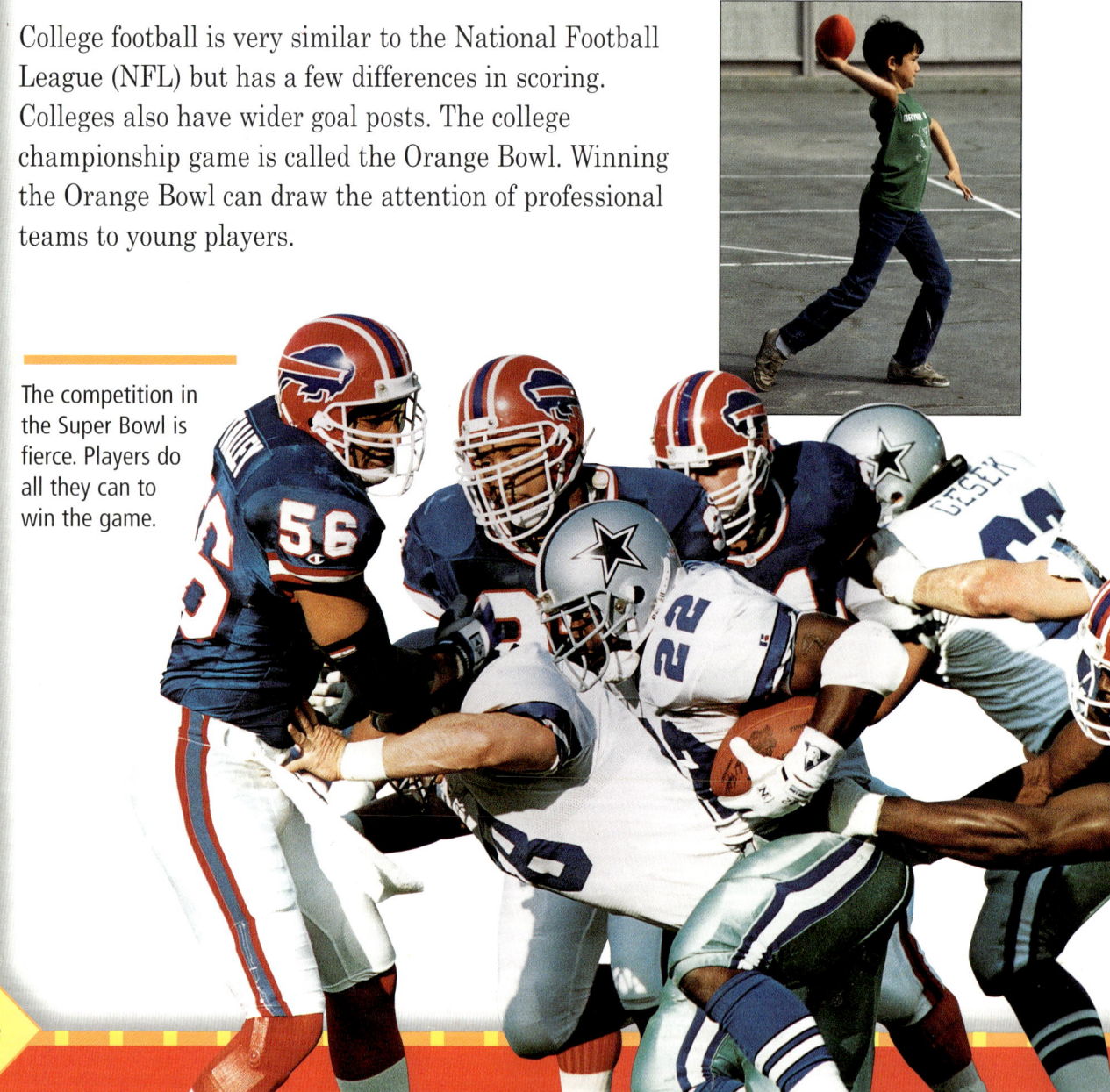

There are different football leagues for college and professional teams. At one point there were both the American Football League (AFL) and the National Football League. Now the NFL is the official league for professional football players in the United States.

Extra players watch the game from the side lines or rest on the bench.

The first championship game in the National Football League took place in Chicago in 1932. In 1969, the championship game became known as the Super Bowl. The Super Bowl is now a famous sporting event that is watched by millions of people across America. The Super Bowl is held in January each year.

Winning college games is very important. It helps players catch the eye of professional scouts.

15

Superstars of the Sport

Football has had many heroes. They were often the inspiration for today's players.

#12 JOE NAMATH

POSITION: Quarterback
TEAM: Los Angeles Rams
SIGNED TO THE NFL: 1965

Career Facts:
- Joe played with the New York Jets until 1976. He played for the Los Angeles Rams the following year.
- Joe was the first player to pass more than 4,000 yards in one season.
- After retiring in 1977, Joe became a successful football broadcaster.
- Joe was named to the AFL All-Star team three times.
- Joe starred in Hollywood movies.

#34 WALTER PAYTON

POSITION: Running Back
TEAM: Chicago Bears
SIGNED TO THE NFL: 1975

Career Facts:
- Walter held the record for rushing, or covering a lot of the field by running and moving the ball forward.
- Walter played for the Bears for twelve seasons and scored 125 touchdowns.
- After his retirement, the Bears retired his number. No other player on that team would ever be able to wear #34 again.
- Walter was voted the NFL Player of the Century by football fans. He was made a member of the Pro Football Hall of Fame in 1993.

#88 LYNN SWANN

POSITION:
Wide Receiver
TEAM:
Pittsburgh Steelers
SIGNED TO THE NFL:
1974

Career Facts:

- Lynn was the number one draft pick.
- In 1993, Lynn was named the Best Athlete of All-time.
- During Lynn's nine professional seasons, he played in four Super Bowls and was named the Most Valuable Player in the Super Bowl twice.
- Lynn holds the Super Bowl records for the most yards gained receiving, at 364 yards, most receptions, with sixteen, and most touchdowns, with three.
- Since 1980, Lynn has been the national spokesperson for the Big Brothers and Big Sisters organizations.
- After retiring, Lynn became a football broadcaster.

#19 JOHNNY UNITAS

POSITION:
Quarterback
TEAM:
Baltimore Colts
SIGNED TO THE NFL:
1956

Career Facts:

- Johnny led the Colts to championship titles in both 1958 and 1959.
- In 1979, Johnny became a member of the Pro Football Hall of Fame.
- Johnny was named the Player of the Year in three separate years.
- Johnny threw at least one touchdown pass in forty-seven straight games.

CHECK IT OUT

To find out more about past football heroes, check out www.profootballhof.com

17

Superstars of Today

The stars of today have fans cheering in the stands every week.

#13 KURT WARNER

POSITION: Quarterback
TEAM: St. Louis Rams
SIGNED TO THE NFL: 1997

Career Facts:
- Kurt started the 1999/2000 season as the backup quarterback. He became a starter when the regular quarterback was injured.
- Kurt won the Most Valuable Player award at the Super Bowl in 2000.
- Before joining the Rams, Kurt worked at a grocery store bagging groceries.
- Kurt started his own career. Instead of being drafted, he walked in and tried out for the team. He surprised everyone when he made it.

#80 JERRY RICE

POSITION: Wide Receiver
TEAM: San Francisco 49ers
SIGNED TO THE NFL: 1985

Career Facts:
- Jerry is considered the greatest wide receiver ever to play football.
- In 1999, Jerry scored 175 touchdowns. This is an NFL record.
- Jerry takes football very seriously. He is one of the best-conditioned players because he follows a very strict training schedule.
- In 1987 and 1990, Jerry won the NFL Player of the Year award.

#21 DEION SANDERS

POSITION:
Defensive Back
TEAM:
Dallas Cowboys
SIGNED TO THE NFL:
1989

Career Fact:

- Deion started his career with the Atlanta Falcons. He was traded to the 49ers in 1993 and then the Cowboys in 1994.
- In 1996, Deion played both cornerback and wide receiver. He was the first football player to do this in more than thirty years.
- Deion played professional baseball at the same time as professional football.
- Deion is expected to break many football records since he retired from baseball and decided to play only football.

#1 WARREN MOON

POSITION:
Quarterback
TEAM:
Kansas City Chiefs
SIGNED TO THE NFL:
1984

Career Facts:

- Warren played for the Houston Oilers until 1993. He then played for the Minnesota Vikings and the Seattle Seahawks. He joined the Kansas City Chiefs after the 1998 season.
- For twenty-two years, Warren has wowed fans of professional football in both the Canadian Football League (CFL) and the NFL. He has played in 321 professional games.
- Warren led the Edmonton Eskimos to five straight Grey Cup victories from 1978 to 1982.

CHECK IT OUT

To find out more about the NFL and its superstars, check out www.nfl.com

19

Staying Healthy

Athletes need to drink a lot of water to replace what their bodies lose through sweat. When muscles are working hard, they produce heat in the body. In order to keep a cool temperature, the body releases heat through sweat.

Athletes also need a healthy diet. Doctors who work in sports medicine say that a healthy diet helps prevent injuries. If an athlete does get injured, a healthy diet encourages bones and muscles to heal faster.

Eating a balanced meal allows athletes to exercise for longer periods of time without getting tired. This means that all athletes should eat meals and snacks from all the different food groups. Foods from different food groups, including fruits and vegetables, milk products, breads and cereals, and protein, have important **nutrients** needed for a healthy body.

Fruit is a good source of vitamins. It gives people quick bursts of energy.

Breads and cereals provide carbohydrates. These nutrients provide the body with energy.

Many athletes enjoy eating big meals the night before a game. Foods such as spaghetti, rice, breads, and vegetables are popular because bodies store them as energy in their muscles. Football players use this energy when they play. It helps them last until the end of the game. To stay healthy on the field, players also stretch and warm up their arms, legs, and back. This helps keep their muscles strong and injury-free.

While meat is important for protein, eating plenty of vegetables helps keep athletes strong and healthy.

Stretching during the pre-game warm-up helps to prevent injury.

CHECK IT OUT
Learn more about eating healthy by visiting
www.sportsparents.com/nutrition/index.html

21

Football Brain Teasers

Test your knowledge of this great sport by trying to answer these football brain teasers!

Q What does NFL stand for?

A NFL stands for National Football League.

Q When is the Super Bowl held?

A The Super Bowl is held in January each year.

Q Do American and Canadian football leagues allow a different number of players on the field at once?

A Yes, there are eleven football players from each team in American football and twelve players from each team in Canadian football.

Q How many yards are between yard lines on a football field?

A Each yard line is five yards apart. A yard is 3 feet long, so the yard lines are 15 feet apart.

Q How long is a football game?

A Each quarter is fifteen minutes long, so a game is one hour long. It takes more than an hour to play because the clock is stopped between plays.

Q Why does a football have laces on it?

A A football has laces to help a player grip the ball when throwing it.

23

Glossary

cleats: special athletic shoes with small spikes or tips on the bottom; they help players stop or turn quickly

contact sport: a sport in which physical contact between players is allowed

down: one of four chances to move the ball 10 yards down a football field

end zone: the end of the field where a touchdown can be scored. The goal posts are in the end zone.

huddle: a small circle of players on the field; plays are discussed in huddles

interception: when a player catches a pass from the opposing team

nutrients: substances needed by the body and obtained from food

possession: control of the ball; being on the offensive

side line: the long part of the field marked by a thick white boundary

spiral: a rotating spin in a football. A spiral helps make the ball go further and land accurately.

tackles: throws or drags down in order to stop advancement

touchdown: scoring by catching or running the ball into the end zone

turf: artificial grass or field made of human-made material

yards: measures of distance on a football field; a yard is equal to 3 feet

Index

down 5, 10
end zone 8, 9, 10, 11, 12
goal post 8, 11, 14
huddle 13
kicking 5, 11
linesmen 13
Moon, Warren 19
Nameth, Joe 16
National Football League (NFL) 14, 15, 16, 17, 18, 19, 22

Orange Bowl 8, 9, 14
padding 6, 7
Payton, Walter 16
quarterback 13, 16, 17, 18, 19
receivers 5, 12, 17, 18, 19
Rice, Jerry 18
rugby 4
Sanders, Deion 19
side line 8, 9, 15
soccer 4

Super Bowl 14, 15, 17, 18, 22
Swann, Lynn 17
tackle 6, 10, 13
touchdown 5, 8, 10, 11, 16, 17, 18
Unitas, Johnny 17
Warner, Kurt 18